TIME
FOR KIDS
READERS

S0-DLD-446

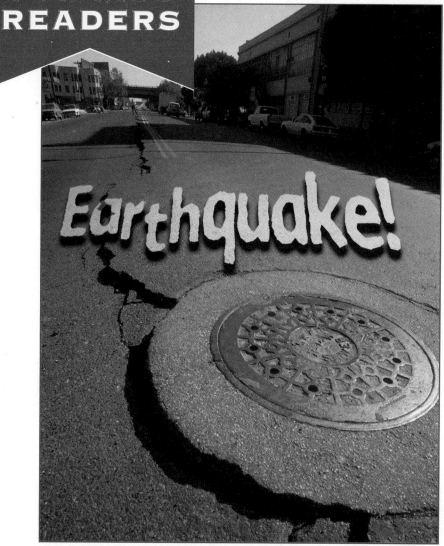

Earthquake!

by Renee Skelton

Harcourt

Orlando Austin Chicago New York Toronto London San Diego

Visit *The Learning Site!*
www.harcourtschool.com

On the night of December 15, 1811, the people of New Madrid, Missouri, went to bed as usual. Everything seemed normal. Then, in the early hours of December 16, the ground began to shake. People were jolted out of bed. Windows rattled. Objects fell off tables and shelves and crashed to the floor. Outside, huge cracks opened in the ground and a roar like thunder filled the air.

The ground under the nearby Mississippi River also shook. Cracks opened and closed in the riverbed. The river swallowed up whole islands. People on boats tried to swim to safety, but many drowned. Many other people drowned on land as riverbanks collapsed and the Mississippi swept in and flooded towns.

Frightened people ran out of their houses. Many of them stayed outside all night in the cold. They were afraid to go back inside. Many people no longer had houses.

A series of earthquakes caused the Mississippi River to swallow up the tiny town of New Madrid, Missouri, in 1812.

As daylight returned on the morning of December 16, people thought the worst was over. Smaller quakes continued for weeks. Then two more big quakes shook New Madrid on January 23 and February 7, 1812. The February 7 quake was the biggest of them all. Most people had already left New Madrid, and the earthquake destroyed what was left of the town. Tiny New Madrid finally disappeared—swallowed up by the river.

The New Madrid quakes shook a large area beyond the town. Shock waves from the quakes destroyed buildings from Cincinnati to St. Louis. Clocks stopped in Savannah, Georgia. Buildings shook and church bells rang in New York City and Boston—more than a thousand miles away. Today, scientists think these earthquakes were among the biggest ever in North America.

The New Madrid earthquakes made these trees tilt.

TFK Spotlight

The San Andreas Fault

Probably the most famous earthquake area in the United States is the San Andreas Fault. The San Andreas Fault is a huge crack that runs more than 800 miles (1,287 km) through the state of California. It's the place where two plates meet and slide past each other. At the San Andreas Fault, the North American plate slides southward, while the Pacific plate slides north. The plates grind along at about 2 inches (5 cm) a year.

Many big California quakes have happened along the San Andreas fault. The 1906 San Francisco earthquake is one of them. It almost destroyed the city. In 1989, the Loma Prieta quake happened south of San Francisco. The quake caused 63 deaths and $6 billion in damage.

In this photo taken from high above California, the cracks caused by the San Andreas Fault can be seen running in a north-south direction.

What is an earthquake? What force is strong enough to make the ground shake? The force comes from Earth itself. An earthquake is caused by giant pieces of Earth moving and rubbing against one another.

The surface of Earth seems as solid as a rock. But we stand only on the outer layer, or crust, of Earth. The crust is cool and hard, but it floats on top of a thick layer of liquid rock called the mantle.

The crust is made up of giant pieces, thousands of miles across. The pieces are called tectonic plates. The plates fit together like pieces of a huge puzzle. There are eight major plates and about two dozen minor ones. The cracks between tectonic plates are called faults. This is where most earthquakes happen.

The tectonic plates move, floating on the mantle beneath them. They creep along very slowly, only inches a year. As they float, the plates bump into one another. Sometimes one plate rides up over another. Sometimes two plates slide past each other in opposite directions. They may even get stuck for a while, pushing against each other.

The plates sometimes get stuck for as long as hundreds of years. During that time, pressure builds up. Imagine the amount of force that a whole section of Earth has as it pushes against another part. That is the massive force of an earthquake. Finally, the pressure becomes too great. The plates suddenly move with tremendous force. That's an earthquake.

A quake sends out waves of energy that travel through Earth's crust. They are called seismic waves. Seismic waves shake the ground and everything on it. The shaking vibrates and causes structures like buildings, bridges, dams, and roads to bounce around. If they shake enough, the structures crack or collapse.

This apartment house in San Francisco, California, was damaged by an earthquake in October 1989.

Earthquake Dos and Don'ts

DO THIS DURING AN EARTHQUAKE

1. If you are indoors, stay there. Duck under a desk or table, go into a hallway, or stand against an inside wall.

2. Keep away from windows, fireplaces, heavy furniture, and large appliances.

3. If you are outside, stay away from buildings, power lines, tall poles, or anything that might fall on you.

4. If you are in a car, stay there. But cars should not stop on or under bridges or highway overpasses, under signs or light poles, or near power lines.

DON'T DO THIS DURING AN EARTHQUAKE

1. Don't use stairs while a building is shaking.

2. Don't turn on the stove or use matches, lighters, camp stoves, electric equipment, or appliances until you are sure there are no gas leaks. They could create a spark that could ignite leaking gas and cause an explosion and fire.

3. Don't use the telephone, except for emergencies. You might tie up the lines.

A scientist at the United States National Seismograph Network holds a printout of below-ground movement. It may show an earthquake has happened—or is coming.

The place where the plate slips or breaks is called the focus of the earthquake. The point on the surface right above the focus is the epicenter. Most quake damage happens at the epicenter. The shaking on the surface is strongest there.

Earthquakes happen every day. Most of them are so small that people cannot feel them, however. The United States has more than 2,500 earthquake monitoring stations. They keep track of every earthquake that happens. To do this, scientists use instruments called seismographs (SYZ•moh•grafs). Seismographs record the movement of rock in Earth's crust.

The monitoring stations are part of the United States National Seismograph Network (USNSN). Each station has seismographs, computers, and other instruments that send information to satellites. These satellites beam the information back down to the National Earthquake Information Center (NEIC) in Colorado.

The NEIC uses the information to find the time, location, and strength of a quake, and the fault that was involved. This happens within minutes of a quake. The NEIC then tells government officials, reporters, and the public that an earthquake has happened.

If the quake was large and in a big city, most people already know. When large quakes happen in faraway areas, information from the NEIC can let people outside the area know what has happened. Officials can rush help to the area, in case people there have been injured.

David McCallen, a scientist, uses a computer program to imitate the effects of an earthquake. Here he studies what could happen to a bridge during an earthquake. The results will help make bridges and buildings safer in the event of future quakes.

Geologists are scientists who study Earth and how it was formed. That makes them experts on earthquakes. In spite of all they know, geologists still cannot predict exactly when an earthquake will occur. However, they can make reasonable guesses as to when and where future quakes might happen. Places near faults or where quakes have occurred in the past are likely spots for new quakes. This knowledge helps people in earthquake zones prepare and protect themselves.

Geologists also study how fast pressure builds up in fault areas. They know that when the pressure becomes too great, the rocks will move and earthquakes will result. Scientists study the past to learn about the present and even the future. How much time passed between earthquakes years ago? What is useful to know about the last quake at a certain fault?

The boundaries of many tectonic plates crisscross Earth. None of these boundaries pass under New Madrid, Missouri.

The answers to those questions allow scientists to figure out the time needed for the strain to build up to a dangerous level.

What caused the New Madrid earthquakes? Present-day scientists asked themselves that question. They knew the history of New Madrid, but they were still puzzled. They looked for clues. For example, they looked at maps that show plate boundaries, or faults. But there are no faults near New Madrid. The geologists then thought there might be a crack in the middle of the plate near New Madrid. They looked and looked, but the ground near New Madrid was not cracked.

It's certain that something caused those earthquakes long ago. It had to be deep under the soil. Geologists used special tools to look at the rock deep below the surface. Then, at long last, they found their answer. The rock was split by a large crack. The scientists named the crack the Reelfoot Rift. A rift is the same as a crack or fault. A layer of soil almost 20 miles (32 km) thick had buried the Reelfoot Rift. This burial took millions of years. The ground at New Madrid shook when rock at the rift moved.

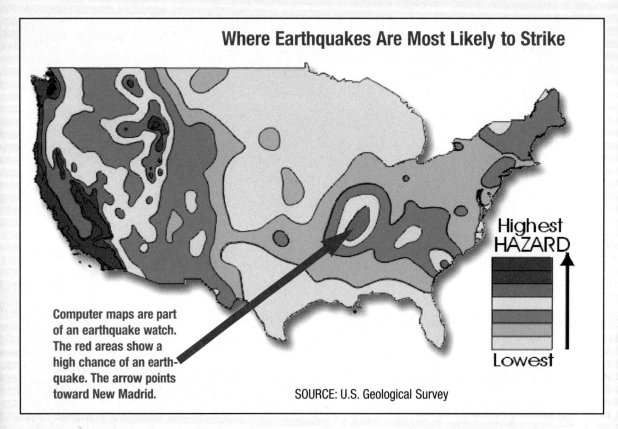

Where Earthquakes Are Most Likely to Strike

Highest
HAZARD

Lowest

Computer maps are part of an earthquake watch. The red areas show a high chance of an earthquake. The arrow points toward New Madrid.

SOURCE: U.S. Geological Survey

Geologists knew the same thing could happen again. The Reelfoot Rift is in an area scientists call the New Madrid seismic zone. The zone contains many smaller faults besides the Reelfoot Rift. The zone extends for about 150 miles (241 km) from northeast Arkansas to southern Illinois. It is about 50 miles (80 km) wide. Most of the earthquakes in the central Mississippi Valley happen within the New Madrid seismic zone.

Geologists also tried to solve another puzzle about the New Madrid quakes. Exactly how big were they? Today scientists have instruments to measure the strength of earthquakes. In 1811, there was no way to measure them.

Many people who were in the area of New Madrid in 1811 wrote about what they saw. Geologists have used these descriptions to try to figure out how strong the quakes were. For example, many people wrote that Earth's surface rolled and cracked. A quake must be very strong to do that. Scientists use the Richter scale to measure and compare the strength of quakes. The eyewitness descriptions tell geologists that the New Madrid quakes were a 7.0–8.0 or more on the Richter scale. They were huge.

Big earthquakes do not often occur east of the Rocky Mountains. When they do happen, they usually cause more damage than quakes in the West. Why? The rock that forms the crust in the East and Midwest is thicker and older than rock in the West. It is more rigid. The rock is also stacked in flatter layers, like a cake. Seismic waves travel much better through this type of rock. They travel longer distances and shake a much larger area.

For example, a big earthquake almost destroyed San Francisco in 1906. That quake was about as strong as the New Madrid quakes. People felt the San Francisco quake 350 miles (563 km) as far away as in Nevada. People felt the New Madrid quakes 1,000 miles (1,609 km) as far away as in Massachusetts.

Much of San Francisco was destroyed by the 1906 quake.

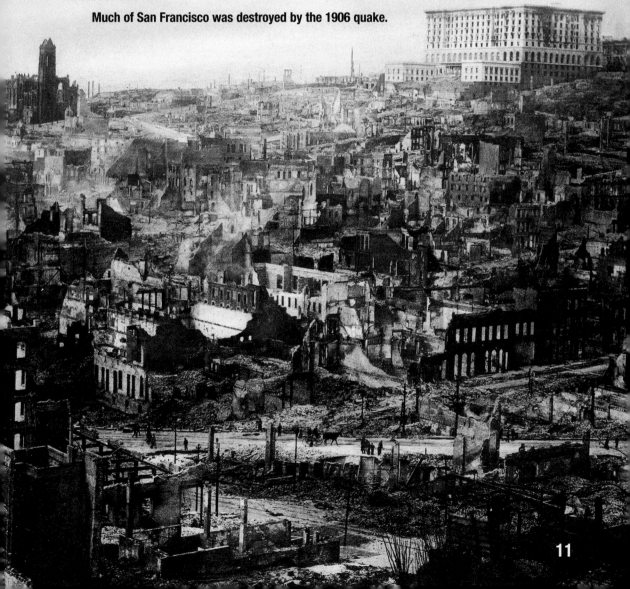

- More earthquakes occur in Alaska than in any other state.
- The largest recorded earthquake in the United States was in March 1964 at Prince William Sound in Alaska. It measured 9.2 on the Richter scale.
- The largest recorded earthquake in the world measured 9.5 on the Richter scale. It happened in Chile on May 22, 1960.
- In the old days scientists must have gotten dizzy. They used huge swinging pendulums to measure the shaking of Earth. The largest pendulum weighed about 15 tons.
- The rock along the San Andreas Fault in California moves about two inches a year. That's about how fast your fingernails grow.
- If the movement along the San Andreas Fault keeps up at the present rate, Los Angeles and San Francisco will be next to each other in about 15 million years.
- Scientific instruments detect about 500,000 earthquakes on Earth each year.
- What do Florida and North Dakota have in common? They have fewer earthquakes than any other states in the United States.
- Antarctica experiences fewer earthquakes than any other continent.

The New Madrid quakes of 1811–1812 were big. But few people died in them, because few people lived there less than 200 years ago. Today, this area has millions of people. A big earthquake could cause destruction in several states, including Illinois, Arkansas, Missouri, Tennessee, and Kentucky. Major damage would also occur in large cities such as St. Louis, Memphis, Louisville, Little Rock, and Cincinnati.

When will the next big earthquake happen in the New Madrid area? No one knows, but it *could* happen. Geologists think there is a 90 percent chance that a big earthquake will happen there in the next 50 years. This quake could knock down buildings and bridges. It could cause fires due to broken gas or power lines. Many people could be hurt or killed. What can be done before then to prevent so much death and destruction?

In places where earthquakes happen often, people know how to prepare for them. Most injuries in earthquakes happen when buildings fall, but there are ways to make buildings that don't fall as easily in earthquakes. The nation of Japan in Asia and our own state of California—both places that experience a lot of quakes—have strict rules about how buildings should be constructed to make them more earthquake-proof.

One way is to make buildings that can bend without breaking. Steel bars in concrete walls help buildings sway slightly in a quake without crumbling.

Another trick is to have a building rest on its foundation but not be attached to it. For example, it might rest on a layer of rubber. That way, when the ground shakes, the building won't shake as much. Also, gas and water pipes can be made with flexible joints so they won't break during a quake. People can also make their homes safer by bolting furniture to the floor or making cabinets and shelves in certain ways so they are earthquake-proof.

Most of the buildings in the New Madrid seismic zone today are not built to withstand an earthquake. Since scientists have predicted that one is coming someday, people are trying to prepare for the danger. New buildings have features that will help them stand up to an earthquake.

In some states, engineers are making highways, bridges, dams, and other structures stronger. Students learn about earthquake safety in school. Government officials in all states in the area have earthquake emergency plans. These plans tell police, firefighters, hospitals, and the public what to do during and after an earthquake.

Repairs are made to a bridge on the day after the 1989 San Francisco earthquake.

Construction workers direct the rebuilding of a California highway after a 1994 earthquake.

TFK
DID YOU KNOW

Earthquakes: By the Numbers

80	Percentage of major earthquakes that occur around the edge of the Pacific Rim
100	Number of earthquakes each year that do great damage
2,600	Number of quakes each day
8,000	Number of small earthquakes that occur somewhere on Earth each day
830,000	Number of people thought to have died in an earthquake in China in 1556—the world's most deadly as of 2002

After the quakes of 1811–1812, people slowly returned to New Madrid. Today, a small town is in almost the same place as the first New Madrid was 200 years ago. Will this small town be the center of another disaster? The people of New Madrid today know a lot more about earthquakes than people did in 1811. They know to expect one and how to prepare for it. With the help of geologists, planners, and other experts, they're hoping the next "big one" won't be a disaster for the people of New Madrid.

How Strong Is an Earthquake?

Most measurements of earthquake force are based on the Richter scale. It was developed in the 1930s by Charles F. Richter. The Richter scale measures the ground motion an earthquake causes.

Earthquakes measured on the Richter scale are rated from one to eight. Each number on the Richter scale represents 32 times greater force than the one before. That means an earthquake that is rated a four is 32 times greater than one rated three.

The Richter scale is good at measuring some kinds of quakes but not all. Other scales have been developed to measure the strength of different types of quakes. The numbers on those scales match the numbers on the Richter scale but scientists use different methods to calculate them. The Modified Mercalli Intensity Scale, for example, measures how strong an earthquake feels to people who are nearby.

A scientist checks a seismograph to see if an earthquake has struck. If it has, he will use the Richter scale to describe its strength.

The Richter Scale

MAGNITUDE	EFFECT OF QUAKE NEAR EPICENTER	ESTIMATED NUMBER EACH YEAR
< 2.5	recorded on seismographs but not usually felt by people	900,000
2.5 – 5.4	felt by many people but causes little damage	30,000
5.5 – 6.0	shocks cause some damage to structures	500
6.1 – 6.9	destruction in built-up areas	100
7.0 – 7.9	major earthquake, causing serious damage (New Madrid quake was this magnitude or higher)	20
> 8.0	strongest earthquakes; causing complete destruction	0.2